LUBNA and PEBBLE

To Lubna and Khadija,
my clever little nieces
across the tumbling
sea. xx

W.M.

For my dear friend
Manal Al Jassim,
a true inspiration.

D.E.

DIAL BOOKS FOR YOUNG READERS
Penguin Young Readers Group
An imprint of Penguin Random House LLC
375 Hudson Street
New York, NY 10014

Text copyright © 2019 by Wendy Meddour
Illustrations copyright © 2019 by Daniel Egnéus

ISBN 9780525554165
Printed in China
1 2 3 4 5 6 7 8 9 10

Design by Cerise Steel
Text set in Two Fingers Bodoni

Lubna
and Pebble

WENDY MEDDOUR

DANIEL EGNÉUS

 Dial Books for Young Readers

Lubna's best friend was a pebble.
It was shiny and smooth and gray.

Lubna found it on the beach when they arrived in the night.

Then she fell asleep in Daddy's salty arms.

When Lubna opened her
eyes, it was morning.

They had landed in
a World of Tents.

Lubna clutched Daddy's
hand and gripped
her pebble.

Somehow, she knew they'd keep her safe.

In a big white tent,
Lubna found a felt-tip pen.

She drew a happy
face on her pebble.

"Hello, Pebble,"
whispered Lubna.

Pebble smiled back.

Lubna told Pebble everything.
About her brothers.
About home.
About the war.

Pebble always listened to her stories.
Pebble always smiled when she felt scared.

"I love you, Pebble," Lubna said with a sigh.

Then, the winter arrived. The winds began to blow.
The tents began to flap.

Daddy said, "Come close,
I'll keep you warm."

But Lubna was worried.
"What if Pebble gets a cold?"

"That must *never* happen," said Daddy.
He went and found a shoe box and a tea towel.

"Thank you." Lubna grinned.

Then she put Pebble to bed and kissed it good night.

Soon, a little
boy arrived.

At first, he had no words.
Just blinks and sneezes
and stares.

"This is my best friend, Pebble,"
Lubna said.

The little boy coughed.
And sneezed.
Then smiled.

"Hello, Pebble.
My name's Amir."

Lubna and Amir became friends.
They played hide-and-seek
underneath the stars.

But at bedtime, Lubna
whispered to Pebble,
"You are *still* my
best friend."

One day,
Daddy was beaming.

"We are leaving.
We have found
a new home!"

Lubna felt happy.
Then sad.

Amir cried.

That night, Lubna couldn't sleep.
She asked Pebble what to do.

Pebble didn't answer.

But by the morning,
Lubna knew.

Lubna gave Amir the shoe
box with Pebble and the pen.

"What do I do if
Pebble misses you?"
asked Amir.

"Draw the smile
back on," said Lubna.

"And what do I do if
I miss you?"

"Tell Pebble all about it," Lubna said.
Amir nodded and held the shoe box tight.

"Good-bye, Pebble,"
Lubna whispered.

"Hello, Pebble,"
Amir said.